AR QUIZ# 170558
BL: 4.9
AR Pts: 2.0

OLD CAT
and the
KITTEN

OLD CAT
and the
KITTEN

Mary E. Little

Aladdin Books
Macmillan Publishing Company • New York
Maxwell Macmillan Canada • Toronto
Maxwell Macmillan International
New York • Oxford • Singapore • Sydney

To all strays,

abandoned pets,

and those who

take pity on them.

First Aladdin Books edition 1994

Aladdin Books
Macmillan Publishing Company
866 Third Avenue
New York, NY 10022

Maxwell Macmillan Canada, Inc.
1200 Eglinton Avenue East
Suite 200
Don Mills, Ontario M3C 3N1

Macmillan Publishing Company is part of the Maxwell Communication Group of Companies.

Printed in the United States of America
10 9 8 7 6 5 4 3 2 1

Library of Congress Cataloging-in-Publication Data
Little, Mary E.
Old Cat and the kitten / Mary E. Little. — 1st Aladdin Books ed.
p. cm.
Summary: Joel faces a difficult decision when he learns that the family is moving and he can't take his adopted tomcat along—abandoning the cat is unthinkable and finding him a new home seems impossible.
ISBN 0-689-71800-4
[1. Cats—Fiction. 2. Pets—Fiction. 3. Moving, Household—Fiction.] I. Title.
PZ7.L72301 1994
[Fic]—dc20 93-30376

CONTENTS

PART ONE

The Old Cat

CHAPTER ONE

HE WAS VERY HUNGRY THE EVENING JOEL FOUND him on the garbage can behind the garage. The pickings were poor for strays, and there were too many strays to pick them.

The old cat had long forgotten what it was like to live instead of just to stay alive. When he was a little kitten, he had been petted and played with and cared for from the time he was chosen out of a litter one spring day.

"He's the prettiest one," the woman had said. "All black with just those little white hairs on his shoulder. Look at those great big yellow eyes! Isn't he cute? Look at the way he grabs my finger! Look at him playing with your shoelace! Oh, he feels so soft against my neck. He'll be company for me when you're back in the city on business."

Until the autumn came and the man said, "We're not taking that cat with us when we leave here. He's old enough now to start spraying around the house."

"We can have him altered—"

"Oh, no. No way! I'm not spending that kind of money on a cat. Besides, he's hardly the pretty little bundle of fluff you picked out, not anymore."

At seven months he was all legs and tail—and appetite.

"Don't freak out so—he'll be all right. Cats can take care of themselves. They're hunters by nature—they can survive."

After they left him, he tried to find somebody else who would feed him and care for him, but he was shooed away, sometimes gently, most of the time not so gently. And if people already had a cat, he was in trouble. The big cats chased him out of their yards, and the small cats made such a fuss if he took their food that some person usually came running out yelling, "Scat!" and going after him with a broom.

So, he had learned to fight the big cats and to keep his distance from people.

As more and more people moved into the neighborhood, the small wildlife worth hunting thinned out and became nearly extinct in this area filled with people, dogs and motor vehicles.

Yet he had survived for over five years—thirty-five in man-years. Now he was worn and raggedy-coated, tired and comfortless. Hunger and fear were all he knew.

When Joel came around the corner of the garage, the old cat leaped from the garbage can and fled halfway down the alley. He stopped halfway because the boy was speaking, and something in the tone of the boy's voice held him.

"Here, Old Cat," Joel called, softly. "I ain't gonna hurt you. Come on, old feller, come on.

You sure look a mess, Old Cat. Come on—come on, let me look at your eye. Come on—come here, don't run."

Joel moved toward the old cat very slowly, holding out his hand, speaking softly, continuously, in a gentle voice. When he was about ten feet away, the old cat snarled and hissed and ran the rest of the way down the alley.

But he came back later that evening and prowled around the garbage can again. The lid was on tight, and powerful as he had become, he could not knock the heavy can over as some dogs are able to do; but he nosed around the bottom of the can, looking for a fallen scrap or two.

When Joel came around the corner of the garage, the old cat ran again, but again at the sound of the boy's voice he stopped and looked back. Joel was carrying a plate with food on it. He came up to the cat slowly, speaking softly, pleading with him.

"Come on back, Old Cat. Come on—you look starved. Come on. Nobody's gonna hurt you. Come on. Come get your dinner. Come on, Old Cat, come on."

The old cat snarled and hissed and ran again as the boy drew near. But once more he stopped and looked back. The smell of the food was an agony, but he'd had experiences with people, with boys and tin cans and rocks and bottles. The puffy scar across his eye and face was the result of a flying piece of glass from a bottle flung at him, that had burst at his running feet. He crouched and hissed and snarled again.

"You sure can swear, can't you, Old Cat. OK. I'll put the plate down here, and you just come eat when you feel like it."

Joel set the plate down close to the fence and backed slowly away, always speaking to the cat. The cat did not move. The smell of the food made him drool, but he did not start toward the plate until the boy was all the way back, peeking around the corner of the garage. Then slowly, fearfully, never taking his eyes off the corner where Joel watched, the old cat crawled on his belly to the plate.

Hunger overcame fear, and he fell on the food, gulping it down as no properly fed cat would ever do. He lifted his head now and then to look warily to each side, then gulped again.

Although he was almost out of sight, Joel kept speaking softly to the cat while it ate.

"Man, you really starving, ain't you. I bet you ain't had a meal like that since Christmas. You gotta come close and let me look at that cut. Your ears is as raggy as your tail. You really a sorry sight, you sure are."

Indeed, the old cat had not had a meal like that for more than a year. His Christmas dinner had been snatched from the edges of garbage cans too full to be tightly covered. The last meal put out for him—just for him—was almost two years ago when, for a few blissful months, an old lady had set a plate for him at her back door. She, too, had talked to him and he had talked back, but even then he had waited until she closed the screen door before he ate. He never let her touch him, but he went to her house every day without

fail until one evening she didn't come to the door at all. He went again, often, faithfully—and hungrily—but he never saw her again.

After the old cat had licked the plate clean the boy, still calling softly, squatted down on his heels and put out his hand again, but even at that distance the movement startled the cat and he ran off down the alley.

Every evening, for almost a week, when Joel came with a plate of food, the old cat jumped off the garbage can where he waited and ran halfway down the alley. Each time the boy set the plate down a little closer to the place where he watched by the corner of the garage, and the cat came and ate, still ravenously, still warily watching and distrustful, but a little nearer to the boy each time.

"You sure cagey, ain't you, Old Cat," the boy crooned. "Guess you had a rough time. Come on, come on, man—don't be scared. Come on—smell my hand. It's a petting hand, see? It's a feeding hand, not a hitting hand. Come on." But the cat would not come to the boy, though he no longer ran away. He raised his head and hissed, then finished his meal.

"You the swearingest cat I ever did see. My mom won't let me swear, not now. She says I gotta be thirteen before I can say damn or hell—that's almost a year off. All I can say now is darn or heck or—aw, come on! Don't go away."

The old cat licked the last bit of food off the plate, then turned his back on the boy. He did not run, but walked steadily away a few paces; then he sat down, and eyeing the boy once more, he began to wash himself.

Joel grinned and slowly sat down on the ground where he'd been squatting.

"That's more like it, Old Cat," he said. "You gonna come to me one of these days. You gonna let me pet you and fix you up. You and me, we gonna be friends."

"Who you talking to? So *that's* where all that good hamburger's been going!"

As the boy's mother pulled him to his feet, the cat ran off down the alley and disappeared.

"Hey, Mom—please! Look what ya done!

You really scared him away! Now I'll have to start all over again, just when he was beginning to listen to me!"

"You listen to me! For the last time: no more animals, you understand? No more!"

"But, Mom–"

"After what I went through with you when your dog got killed? No–no more pets!"

"Mom, listen–"

"*You* listen! I come home all done in from work, on my feet all day at the beauty shop, and what do I find? The Fiends mauling each other and you outside here feeding my hard-earned food to a filthy stray cat!"

"But Mom, if I take care of him a little, he'll–"

"Cats can take care of themselves. Now get in there."

"But he's starving and hurt. He needs help."

"*I* need help–and you got a little brother and sister in the house needs help. Now move. Get those kids washed and put to bed while I fix me something to eat–if there's any food left!"

CHAPTER TWO

THE TOWN LAY IN A VALLEY NEAR A LAKE THAT was bordered by summer cottages, some of which were owned by the wealthier townsfolk. Others served as vacation homes for summer visitors. On one side of the town an old, unused railway station was edged by rows of small, identical houses, each with its narrow driveway and a single-car garage on the alley behind it. It was in one of these houses that Joel lived with his mother and little stepbrother and sister. His stepfather had left them there a year ago to look for work in the city some hundred or so miles away. Joel could not really remember his own father, but he cherished a snapshot of him in his army sergeant's uniform, sent home shortly before his death in Vietnam.

It was not easy for a boy to find a money-earning job in this town. People did what they could for themselves in the way of chores, and what jobs there were went to teen-agers and adults. Joel received a small weekly allowance from his mother, but it didn't stretch very far and he had been saving all he could spare for a microscope, not one of those toy things but a real microscope that would last him through high school—maybe even college if he could ever get that far. His friend Wayne had told Joel he'd seen a good second-hand one in the city for eighty dollars. That was a lot of money, but he'd managed to save almost eighteen dollars since Christmas.

Now that he'd made a deal with his mother about the old cat, he'd have to earn some money, because part of the deal was that he'd have to feed the cat on his own—from his own plate or out of his own pocket. After a bang-up row the night before, he and his mother had come to terms: she promised to let him fix a shelter for the old cat in the garage. The spring rains were not over and the winds off the lake could be very cold. She seldom promised him anything; but when she did, she kept her promise, he could say that for her. But she knew how to drive a hard bargain. He had also to baby-sit, without complaining, from the time the Fiends were brought home from nursery school by another mother, until she got home from work.

The next morning she gave him a piece of old blanket.

"You can make a bed for that old cat back there on the floor in the corner of the garage."

"Not on the floor, Mom. Cats like little boxes or high places."

"Then hang him on the chandelier—and provide your own chandelier. Just keep him out of the house. I'm warning you, don't you ever let me catch that animal in the house."

She got into the car, where the Fiends were

already roughhousing in the back seat, and put her key in the ignition.

"I got to get these Fiends to nursery school before they pull each other's clothes off. Don't you be late to school, now, fooling around over that old cat."

She started to back out of the driveway, then rolled her window down for a last word.

"I just don't understand. You always so particular. What you want, anyway, with a beat-up old specimen like that? Now if it was a pretty, clean little kitten . . ."

Joel folded the piece of blanket and laid it on the tool shelf, then he came up to the driver's side of the car.

"He was a pretty, clean little kitten once, Mom," he said. "Ain't his fault nobody gave him a home. I wonder . . . I wonder if he ever had a home at all. Maybe somebody, summer visitors maybe, took care of him when he was little and cute and then when he got to be big and kinda awkward they banded him—"

"*Abandoned*, stupid. When you gonna begin to talk like you had some education? *Abandoned*, not *banded*."

She backed the rest of the way out of the driveway.

"Behave yourself—have a good day," she called.

"You too, Mom," he answered.

As soon as she had turned and pulled off down the street, he hurried to the back of the garage, picking up a hammer and chisel from the tool shelf on the way.

Only when a big storm was forecast was the car ever put in the garage. Like most of the others in this block, the car stayed closed and locked in the driveway, and the garage was used as a place to store things for which there was no room in the house. Most of the things lined around the sides and back of the garage belonged to Joel, who had no room of his own. He had found sharing a small bedroom with the Fiends a greater trial than sleeping on the living room sofa and keeping his belongings in the garage. At the back stood an old dining room sideboard, part of which could be locked, and only he had the key for it. Above this was a tiny window, which, on the alley side, was just over the big garbage can.

This little window was so covered with dirt and cobwebs that no one ever noticed that it had been broken and part of the pane was missing; no one except Joel, who now stood up on top of the sideboard and began to hammer out the rest of the glass. He made a neat job of it, then he took a brush and dust pan and cleared away all the broken glass in the garage and in the alley.

If only he could encourage Old Cat to use this for a cat hole, then he'd buy a piece of plexiglass and tape it at the top so that it could swing both ways, and Old Cat could come and go from the alley as he pleased.

Joel quickly tidied up, grabbed his lunch off the kitchen counter, straddled his bicycle and pedaled away with joyful speed to school.

He worked very hard that afternoon at baby-sitting the Fiends. He read them a story and then made them some creepy-crawlies. He didn't even slip out once while they were watching television. He cooked their hamburger very carefully. He heated a can of mixed vegetables, poured their milk and tried to keep three-year-old Bitsy from knocking hers over. He failed, cleaned up the mess and poured out more. Four-year-old Seth had, as usual, picked all the carrots out of his vegetables and didn't want to eat the rest. But after a tiresome game of counting the pieces left over—until there were none—Joel gave them their chocolate pudding, and they were being bathed when their mother came home. She took over, and he was free at last to seek out the old cat.

He was glad he had spent twenty-nine cents for a can of cat food. He'd had no idea that cat food cost so much, and he hoped he could get a job before he used up all his money. He hated the thought of chipping away at his microscope money.

His mother objected to his feeding the cat off a plate, so he emptied the cat food onto the lid of a plastic cottage cheese container and set off for the alley.

Remembering the disaster of the night before, he wondered if the cat would come back. He approached the corner of the garage quietly and began to speak slowly, softly.

"Come on, Old Cat. I can take care of you now, Old Cat. Come on, be my cat, Old Cat. Come on, we gonna be friends like I said. Come . . ."

Old Cat was lying across the top of the garbage can, staring at the corner of the garage, waiting. When Joel appeared there, the cat drew himself into a crouch, still watching, ready to spring. But he did not spring.

There was a moment of total silence, of complete stillness, as boy and cat looked at each other.

It was Old Cat who broke the silence, with his usual hiss.

"Man! Am I glad to see you," Joel crooned. The cat answered with a low growl, eyes still fixed on the boy.

"Look here, Old Cat. I brought your dinner —something special just for cats. Costs twenty-

nine cents so it ought to be good."

The cat answered. Joel found it wholly delightful that every time he spoke, the cat answered.

"Man! If only you could speak English," he said. "I'd sure like to know what you're saying. I'd sure like to know what's that swear-word you start out with. Sounds like 'hell' to me, but you probably got a better one, even."

He kept all his movements slow and his voice soft and crooning. He held out the plate toward Old Cat. The cat would not come, but continued to "talk."

"OK. I read you." Joel put the plate on the ground and stepped back a few paces, then sat down, knees drawn up. Old Cat jumped down from the garbage can and began to eat hungrily; no more talking on his part.

"That's a nasty-looking scar you got, Old Cat. Sure is ugly—makes you look like a real hood. You no beauty to begin with, and that puffy scar makes you look downright evilish. You'd scare the pants off an angel."

Old Cat licked the plate clean, then sat where he was and washed himself. When Joel slowly reached out a hand to try to touch him, the cat shrank away from it and got to his feet. He turned his back and walked calmly, tail up, away down the alley.

CHAPTER THREE

EVERY EVENING JOEL FOUND OLD CAT WAITING on the garbage can. When it rained, he put down a large brown carton and set the plate of food inside it so that cat and food were sheltered during the meal.

Then one evening Joel decided to stand—or sit—his ground. Instead of backing away he put the plate down and sat down beside it.

"It's about time you let me stay to dinner, Old Cat. It's about time. Here I been feeding you all this time, buying your dinner out of my own money, serving it all up your way. Least you can do is eat beside me. I won't touch you—not yet."

After a while Old Cat, still growling a little, found that his hunger overcame his distrust, and he ate his food within inches of Joel's hand.

Joel was very careful not to make any further motions toward Old Cat other than leaving his hand lying, relaxed, beside the dish. Old Cat sniffed the hand. He decided it held no threat to him and ignored it until one evening, suddenly, before he touched the food, Old Cat sniffed those fingers again. Then he pressed his forehead against Joel's wrist. Gently, the boy turned his hand and his fingers stroked Old Cat's chin. They moved slowly under his ear, but when Joel tried to stroke his head Old Cat drew back.

"OK, Old Cat—I'll let you do all the making up. I'll just go along with you. OK, you just show me—show me Old Cat. Show me how you want it—show me, show me."

His hand lay still once more. Again Old Cat pressed his forehead against the boy's arm.

And Joel felt his throat swell, and he had to

stop his crooning and fight back the sudden tears in his eyes as Old Cat butted his forehead all along his arm, rubbed it and pressed it along his side, in his armpit, against his chest. Then the cat stretched out on the ground and rolled over on his back and squirmed from side to side; and this time when Joel put his hand under Old Cat's chin, the cat's front paws, claws sheathed, closed over it; his hind feet came up close together and beat gently, rapidly, playfully against Joel's arm.

Joel swallowed.

"I told you we was gonna be friends, didn't I?" he whispered. "You and me, we gonna have a ball, that's what we gonna have, you and me. I'm your man, and you my Old Cat, right? My Old Cat, my Old Cat."

At last Old Cat left off his loving and turned to his dinner, but now he let Joel stroke him while he ate. When the cat had finished and washed, Joel stood up.

"You gonna stay here now and live in my garage? You gonna sleep in that nice bed I made

for you, huh? You gonna stay, Old Cat? This a good place I fixed for you, come on, come on."

Old Cat rubbed his body against the boy's ankles, weaving in and out between his feet. With his tail and hindquarters pressed against Joel's knee, he rubbed his scarred face on Joel's foot until he lost his balance and turned over in a complete somersault.

"You old comedian you!" Joel laughed as he rubbed Old Cat's tummy. "You still got fun in you, haven't you, Old Cat? Even after all you been through, poor old guy. Here, let me look at that scar."

He knelt beside the cat and peered closely at the puffy scar that ran down the eyebrow, over the eye and across the cheek.

"That eye don't look so good, old fella. It's looking kinda cloudy, like a scum starting over it. Wish I knew what to do—jeez, I wish I knew."

After more petting, Joel tried to get Old Cat to come to the garage window. He went around and inside the garage and brought back the piece of old blanket. He let the cat smell it, sniff it thoroughly all over, then he stood up on the garbage can and reached through the window and dropped the blanket to the top of the sideboard. When Old Cat did not appear anxious to follow it through the window, Joel went back inside the garage and stood up on the old sideboard. He let Old Cat see him through the window and called, "Come on, Old Cat. Come on in, Old Cat. Come on, see your own place, your own sleeping place, nice and cozy in here. Come on."

Old Cat jumped up on the garbage can and then into the window and balanced on the windowsill. He did not join Joel on the sideboard, however, but turned around and jumped back out into the alley.

He simply did not show any interest in the shelter, and finally Joel joined him in the alley again.

"Guess I'll have to let you have your own way, as usual," Joel sighed. "I sure hope you'll stay around. I sure hope you'll let me know, some way, what you want."

But after a while, when it was almost dark,

with a new moon rising over the trees around the lake and stars coming out thickly across the sky, Old Cat turned his back on Joel and walked with graceful dignity away down the alley.

Every evening after that Joel and Old Cat spent a longer time together as though they measured out their time by the lengthening of the days. Joel tried to interest the cat in a string or a ball, but Old Cat seemed to want nothing but affection. It was as though he had stored within himself so much unused love that now he could not hold it in. If Joel sat down, Old Cat was in his lap at once, nestling in his arms, pawing with sheathed claws, burying his head under Joel's armpit or in the crook of his arm, licking Joel's skin. He did not talk much any more, except when he first arrived, asking for his dinner, but he purred almost from the time he came until the time came when he decided he must go. Then he walked away, always in the same direction, always slowly now, tail up and strangely beautiful.

Along the fence across the alley someone had planted the kind of roses that grow in trailing clusters. They were now in full bloom falling over the fence and tangling in an overgrowth of weeds and tall grass that grew at the alley's edge. As Old Cat walked past he always brushed against them as though enjoying their scent, their softness, their color. And sometimes cat and roses were washed with moonlight and made a picture that Joel would never forget.

PART TWO

Old Cat and the Kitten

CHAPTER ONE

OLD CAT WALKED DOWN THE ALLEY INTO THE next block and crawled under a crumbling stucco wall. Several of the houses in this block were old. This one was very old and long vacant, and what had once been a rock garden and lily pond in its back yard was now a catchall for trash. An old wheelless baby carriage lay on its side on top of a heap of cast-off furniture, broken tools, rusted auto parts, a twisted metal garden chair and other junk, and because it had all piled up on top of the rocks, there was a small opening underneath that made a shelter of sorts. Early in April, a mother cat had had a litter of four—three gray and one black. They had nested in the overturned baby carriage on the top of the heap. Old Cat stayed in the shelter below.

Then the rains had started, and after a few weeks, the shelter had filled with water. Old Cat had had to move. He had nosed around the pile and found that the baby carriage was empty, so he moved in. It was damp and smelly, but better than the wet shelter under the pile. If the sun came out, a bit of it reached the ragged mattress during the afternoon and he could warm himself a little before he set out for the evening.

He was alone until early one morning when he was awakened as what seemed to be a part of him began to move up and down his belly, nuzzling and biting. The hair rose along his backbone, and he growled. He nosed the thing, and it curled itself into a small ball under his chin, mewing miserably.

It was the black kitten, about six or seven weeks old. She was wet, and her downy fur was caked with chunks of mud. Again, she nuzzled along Old Cat's underside. He got to his feet and arched his body over her, growling, but she went on, stretching up, hungrily nibbling at his belly. He pushed her away with his forehead and held her down with one great black paw. Then he crouched over her and, starting with her face, he began to lick. His big, rough tongue worked steadily in and out of her ears, around her neck, over her head, and she relaxed and stopped her pitiful, sharp mewing. She was quiet as he licked her clean.

He was not hungry when, at dawn, he had crawled into the baby carriage to sleep. Now, however, he got up, stretched and started to leave. The kitten tumbled after him, but he cuffed her back into the nest.

When he returned, he carried in his mouth a broken-off piece of stale cookie, which he dropped in front of the kitten. She licked at it and batted it with her tiny paws. Some of the broken edges crumbled off and softened, and she licked them away. Old Cat lay and watched her.

When the kitten gave up on the hard cookie, she nuzzled Old Cat again, biting at his underside in search of real nourishment. He stood up, arched, and when she continued to try to nurse, he cuffed her off. Then he left the nest again.

This time, when he returned, he carried a strip of gristle with fat, but no meat on it. The kitten sucked at it for a while, then gave up and once again attacked Old Cat's belly. He paid no attention and chewed on the gristle himself. This bit of food had been cleverly come by, snatched from a mongrel's dish while the dog was chasing off another cat.

When Old Cat had done all he could with the gristle, he tried to do what he could with the nest, now foul with kitten droppings. There was not much left of the old carriage mattress, but he pawed and scraped and kicked with his hind feet until some of the dirt was out of the nest. After this, he washed himself, fending off the kitten with his nose or cuffing her away until he had finished. Then he stretched out flat and reached for the kitten with both paws. He washed her thoroughly all over. It was now midmorning, and when the kitten finally lay still beneath his paws, he lowered his chin over her and slept, too.

It was not easy for an old, worn-out fighting tom to mother a little kitten, but he tried. His best source of food for the kitten was the loaded dish belonging to the mongrel dog nearby, and he really enjoyed fooling the young animal by luring him to one end of the fenced-in yard, then dashing in and grabbing from the plate whatever he could carry away in his mouth. He usually jumped to the top of the fence and showed off his loot, while the dog barked insanely and flung himself against the boards below.

Unfortunately, the kind of food he was able to carry was seldom anything that the kitten could eat. Even if he had wished to share with her the food given to him by the boy, it was never of the kind he could carry a distance of two blocks, being either a soft, moist mixture or hard crumbly particles. A small frog now and then, or a field mouse gave the kitten her best nourishment, but there were not enough of these around. Also, he did not know how to teach her to find the food for herself. Slowly she began to lose her strength. She no longer tried to follow him, or nuzzle or play about the nest.

As the kitten weakened, Old Cat brought more and more odds and ends until the nest was foul with bits of stale and rotting food.

When Old Cat could no longer bear this state of affairs, he pushed the kitten out of the nest all the way down to the ground. There he washed her and tried to get her to follow him out to the alley. He had some trouble getting her under the stucco wall and, once out on the alley side, she lay down and refused to move. He sat beside her, but when a large stray dog came excitedly toward them he rose. With hair standing out on body and tail until he appeared to be twice his size, he arched his back. Hissing and snarling, he moved toward the dog, who halted, whined, then turned around and ran back the way he had come.

After a while, Old Cat nudged the kitten to her feet. She wobbled after him for a few paces,

then lay down again. He mouthed her all over, trying to pick her up, but she mewed and cried and squirmed away from him. At last, he got hold of her at the back of the neck and lifted her by her skin. She stopped struggling then, and he carried her up the alley.

CHAPTER TWO

"WHERE YOU, OLD CAT? YOU LATE TONIGHT. Come on, Old Cat—come get your dinner. Come on, Old Cat, come on."

Old Cat came out from under a cluster of roses and twined around Joel's ankles. He set the heaping plate down on the ground and stroked Old Cat's head.

"This here's a special dinner tonight, Old Cat," he said. " 'Special Deluxe Dinner' it's called. It's got chicken and liver and egg and kidney—that's what it says on the label. What's the matter,

Old Cat–ain't you hungry? Don't you like that dinner? What's the matter?"

Old Cat sat beside the plate of food, but he neither sniffed nor tasted it. He just sat there and looked down the alley at the cluster of roses.

"What you looking at, Old Cat? Huh? What you–what the he– what the heck is *that*?"

The cluster of roses moved, and the black kitten came out from underneath. She swayed, then took a few steps toward them and sat down. She got up and moved a few more steps, then stumbling, wobbling all the way, she finally got herself to the plate and sank her face into the food. She put both paws into the plate and pressed them one after the other into the food as she sucked it up.

"Golly! I never seen anything like that before. Hey–she's gonna choke herself! Hey, there, wait a minute, kitty. Slow up there–you gonna be sick."

Old Cat sat still beside the plate, not touching it nor the kitten, just watching as Joel knelt down and gently lifted the kitten away from the food. All four legs were waving, tiny toes spread out, reaching toward the food. He set her back again.

"Old Cat, you been fooling me all along? You been fooling me? No–no, you ain't no mother cat. I know an old tom when I see one."

The boy stroked Old Cat while they both watched the kitten eat.

"That sure your baby, though–even got those white hairs on her shoulder. How come, Old Cat? How come? I sure never heard tell of a male cat taking care of a kitten, his or any other –hey, wait! I told you–"

The kitten began to choke, and as Joel lifted her away from the plate she threw up. "See? That's what you get for being so greedy, see? Only–you ain't greedy, you just plain starved. What you need is some milk."

He stroked the black kitten nestled against his chest.

"You stay here, Old Cat. I gotta see what I can do."

Old Cat followed the boy, for the first time,

to the back door of the house.

Instead of going in, Joel rattled the screen door and called softly.

"Mom—hey, Mom! Can you come to the back door a minute?"

"What you want? I'm busy."

"Mom, is the Fiends asleep yet?"

"Not for long if you keep up that racket."

"Mom, *please*!"

She came to the door, and Old Cat moved a few feet away, crouching.

"Oh! For lord's sake! What now!" She opened the screen door and came outside peering at the kitten.

"Mom, Old Cat brought her. She needs some milk—please. I'll pay you back tomorrow."

"I thought you told me that old cat was a tom?"

"He is."

"Then what the hell's he doing with a kitten? Don't you go taking advantage of me, boy! Just because I let you keep that old cat don't mean I'm going to put up with any litter–"

"Mom, please! Please listen."

The only light came from the kitchen and from a half-risen moon. Joel held the kitten out with both hands so that his mother could see it better.

"Mom, he led this kitten–Old Cat brought her–just this one–to the food tonight. He ain't touched the food himself. She gobbled it, then threw it up because it's too much for her. She needs milk, Mom, and–and maybe baby food. But right now, mostly she needs milk. Please, Mom–see? She's really starving."

His mother took the kitten into her hands.

"You right about that, son. I never seen anything this thin. You don't really think you gonna keep her alive, do you?"

"I gotta try Mom–I just got to–after the way Old Cat brought her–like he knew I'd take care of her. Mom, I just can't *not* try to save her –please . . ."

He noticed with surprise, and hope, that his

mother was stroking the kitten.

"You got your work cut out for you with this one. Nothing this thin could ever survive. But, I have to hand it to you, son, you sure done wonders with that old tom. If it wasn't for that ugly face of his all screwed up with that scar, he'd be a handsome animal."

The boy wondered if his mother knew how gently she was cradling the kitten.

"Your brother left half his milk on the kitchen table—it won't be too cold like what's in the refrigerator. You can use one of them pink saucers tonight, but you'll have to find something else to feed her with tomorrow."

When he came back out with the brimming saucer, his mother dipped her fingers in the milk and rubbed them against the kitten's mouth. Then they both knelt to watch while the kitten waded in and began to drink. Old Cat relaxed and lay quietly where he was, watching.

"Where you going to put them? You say the old cat don't use the place you went to all that trouble to fix up for him."

"I don't know." Joel sighed. "I don't think I can put them anywhere. I just have to wait and let Old Cat show me what he wants. It's his kitten. I guess he'll let me know what he wants, when he's ready."

CHAPTER THREE

"WISH YOU'D LISTEN TO ME SAME WAY YOU LET that Old Cat boss you around," Joel's mother said later as they were putting away the supper dishes and setting the kitchen table for breakfast. They had watched the kitten fill herself until her sides were stretched out, then stagger over to Old Cat who held her between his paws and washed her clean. Joel had brought another plate of food and set it down beside Old Cat, who then ate hungrily while the kitten slept. Then Joel and his mother went into the house, leaving cat and kitten in the yard.

Joel set the box of cold cereal in the middle of the table. "That's just the way cats are," he told his mother. "You got to help them—they independent, but they got to have people-help, too. Only you got to let them decide. Say, Mom—how come—how come you knew how to get that kitten to lap milk?"

"You heard me tell you a hundred times: I lived for a while in the country when I was a little kid." She sat down at the table and hooked a foot around another chair pulling it out so she could put her feet up on it. "Lord, I'm tired," she said, lighting a cigarette. The boy sat in the chair across from her and crossed his arms on the table. He waited while she puffed again on her cigarette.

"We had cats—sometimes lots of cats, and kittens. They lived out in back, in the barn, and they were wild. Sometimes, when one of the old cats had kittens, I'd get to feed them, but mostly they fed themselves. Sometimes I'd pick one out for my own special pet, but my mom never let me bring it in the house, and it would run wild, then, with the rest. Oh, I used to want one so bad, just my own kitten to take care of and play with, but Mom never let me."

She stopped, and she and Joel looked deeply at each other. He said nothing. Then she went on.

"Once I tried to pick one up too soon after it was born, and the old mamma cat jumped up and scratched and bit me. I was a bloody mess and screaming my head off, and Mom came running out and carried me inside. She put some stuff on my bites and scratches that hurt something awful and made them bleed a lot more. But she was mad. 'Don't you ever mess around with cats again, you hear me?' she yelled. 'Now you see what they like. They cute and pretty when they little, but they grow up—kittens gets to be cats, and cats is mean and vicious. All they good for is to keep the place clean of rats and mice.' "

She pulled on her cigarette again. Joel still said nothing.

"We moved back to the city soon after that. One of the kids in my class at school had a cat,

and I used to go to her house and play with it. It was black, with white around its face and on its chest and paws. It was sweet and gentle and when it had kittens there was one just like it, and the girl said I could have it. I begged and begged, but Mom wouldn't let me. I never had a pet of my own."

"You got one now, Mom. You got a kitten if you want it."

She pulled her feet down off the chair and stood up.

"You kidding?" she said, grinding out her cigarette in the sink. "That poor thing won't last a week. Anyway, you wouldn't want to risk its life with them two, now would you?" She jerked her head in the direction of the little bedroom.

"Well—we'd sure have to watch them, make sure—but Mom." He got up and stood beside his mother at the sink. "It might not be such a bad idea. They got to learn. Kids ought to learn how to treat little things, 'specially if they's helpless. They got to learn that animals feel, same as they do. And if you love them they'll love you back."

He followed her into the living room and switched on the television, careful to turn down the volume.

"Those two," he went on. "They sure a awful nuisance, but they ain't mean. They could learn—it might be good for them."

"I'm too tired—let's get ready for bed—we'll talk about it tomorrow."

Joel said no more and switched off the television, but he smiled to himself as he made up his bed on the sofa. His alarm clock was set as usual for quarter past six. He reset it for midnight.

After his mother went to her room, he went back into the kitchen. He poured milk from the refrigerator into a small glass jar and found a chipped saucer containing a soap pad under the sink. He washed the saucer out and dried it and set it beside the glass jar, then he stopped with his hand on the refrigerator door. What the heck—he'd lined up a job for Saturday mornings when Louella, the teen-ager next door, baby-sat for them. (He was tall for his age; when he told the manager he was thirteen going on fourteen he got the job. That was only a part-lie; after all, he *would* be thirteen going on fourteen in ten month's time.) So he could pay.

He took out an egg and broke the yolk into the milk, then he stirred it, screwed the cover on the jar and shook it. He climbed up on a chair and searched the top shelf of the pantry cupboard. Sure enough, he found several little jars of baby food, saved for use if one of the children was sick. There was applesauce, spinach–not much good for cats–but behind these were several jars each of lamb and turkey and beef and liver and egg yolk. He brought some of these down within easy reach, then he turned off the light and went back to the living room. He took off his shoes, but lay down, still dressed, on the sofa, arms crossed over his chest. It was not until some time later that he turned over on his stomach and finally went to sleep.

He wondered where Old Cat had taken the kitten. At midnight the back yard was bright with moonlight, but he could not find them anywhere. He went to the side of the garage and began to call, softly, so as not to wake anyone in the house.

"Come on, Old Cat—come get your dinner, Old Cat, Old Cat. Come on, Old Cat, come on."

In the alley he went toward the roses, and with his foot he carefully moved the heavy clusters, which reached the ground, but there was no cat or kitten underneath.

Disappointed and puzzled, not knowing what to do or where else to look, he turned back the way he had come. As he reached the corner of the garage, Old Cat came toward him from the driveway.

"Where you been, Old Cat? Where you got that kitten? What you done with her, hey?" His hands were too full to stroke Old Cat as he rubbed around Joel's ankles. "Don't you trip me, Old Cat. Show me where that kitten is. She got to eat some more. Come on, show me. Show me, Old Cat."

He had to step slowly because Old Cat kept rubbing around his ankles, making walking difficult. When he reached the driveway, Joel set the things down and squatted, stroking Old Cat.

"What you done with that kitten, Old Cat? Where is she, huh? Where . . ."

From somewhere within the garage came the sad, sharp cry of the kitten.

Joel walked to the back of the garage to where the sideboard stood below the little window. There was just enough room underneath it for the piece of old blanket, pulled down from the place where the boy had so carefully laid it for Old Cat. It made a soft bed for the kitten, who lay there now, awake and hungry.

"You old comedian, you!" Joel said with affection. "You wouldn't stay where I fixed it all up for you—you had to go pull it down so the kitten—"

He suddenly thought of something else. While the kitten was lapping up the egg and milk, he searched the garage until he found a large tin cookie box containing odds and ends, mostly small, broken parts of things. He removed the lid, which was about three-quarters of an inch deep, and carried it out to the back yard where he scooped up enough sand from the Fiends' sandpile to fill it, then he took it back and set it beside the kitten's nest in the garage. When the kitten had finished eating, he would set her in it and hope she'd learn what it was for.

But here Old Cat took over.

That lid was much too small for Old Cat to use, and his efforts to fit on it, turning and scratching and trying to make himself small enough to keep his hindquarters inside, were marvelous to see. He worked very hard and finally managed to squat so that some of his excretion went into the lid. He was so pleased and satisfied with himself that he scratched and kicked most of the sand out of the lid, and Joel had to sweep it up and put it back into the tiny litter box.

Thinking about Old Cat, Joel kept awake, laughing, long after he got back to his sofa, and the next morning it was difficult for him to describe it all to his mother.

"You never seen anything so funny, Mom," he sputtered. "He'd turn and squat and then decide he was going to miss, then he'd turn and squat again. And the funny thing, Mom—the funny thing, I don't think he really had to go at all. I think he was just trying to get it ready for the kitten."

"Did it work?" she asked. "Did the kitten use it when you put her in?"

"*I* didn't put her in, Mom—*he* did. Old Cat shoved her into the box and wouldn't let her out 'til she did something. And you know what, Mom? I think that shows that somebody showed *him* a litter box once. Like I said—pro'bly when he was little and cute somebody took care of him. And then for some reason they—they abandoned him."

He took hold of his mother's arm.

"Mom, you got to promise me—promise me, Mom, you won't ever abandon that little kitten—even when she grows up."

"Grows up? We don't even know if she's gonna make it 'til bedtime."

"Yes, she is. She's gonna make it all right—you should see her eat. She's gonna be all right, Mom. Promise me—please."

She didn't answer him immediately. It was

true that if she promised anything, she kept her promise. Therefore, she never made a promise until she was sure of keeping it.

"We'll see," was all she said. Then "Come on, now, help me get the Fiends ready for nursery school."

PART THREE

The Boy

CHAPTER ONE

ONCE THE RAINY SEASON WAS PAST, SUMMER moved in early. The air was delicious with the fragrance of roses and honeysuckle and fresh-cut grass, and the many small sweet blossoms of roadsides and flowerbeds. Summer cottages were being opened and aired and readied for long weekends and vacations. The lake now sparkled with sailboats and buzzed with motorboats; and there were some eager swimmers already diving into its crisp waters, Joel among them.

In his free time, Joel spent the sunny hours

with his friends, fishing, swimming, bicycling around the lake. And at the end of the long warm days there was Old Cat, now, to come home to: Old Cat and the kitten. His mother had taken the kitten into the house, and she and Joel had carefully taught the Fiends how to handle her. Bitsy was surprisingly gentle. She loved to have the kitten sleep with her in her bed, never knowing that as soon as she fell asleep the kitten was put outside with Old Cat. A litter box was placed for the kitten under the washbasin in the bathroom, and sometimes she was allowed to play indoors during the day. Seth quickly learned that kitty scratched if he teased her, so he was never rough with her and soon lost interest. He really liked his little racing cars better than he liked the kitten.

Old Cat was never allowed to set foot in the house, but then he never seemed to want to. He waited patiently outside the back door until the kitten was brought out.

Joel was worried about Old Cat's eye, and one day he unlocked the sideboard in the garage and took out from one of the wide, flat drawers

a big, beautiful book with full-color photographs. The short text was about the different breeds and the history of cats and their behavior. There was very little on cat care and nothing on treatment or medication except the advice to "see your veterinarian." There was only one picture of strays.

The book was from the public library and was so long overdue that Joel had been afraid to take it back. He had borrowed the book two years ago when he was little, but old enough to remove the overdue notices from the mail before his mother could see them, and they were there inside the cover of the book: two postcards and a bill for six dollars and ninety-five cents. The book was in good condition; he had simply loved it so much he couldn't bear to take it back. He had hoped that some day he could pay the library for it as a "lost" book. He'd heard of kids doing that so they could keep the book and use their library cards again.

He had also heard that the librarian was "easy." Now he hoped that if he returned the book and paid a part of the fine—he didn't know how much it would be for such a long time—maybe she would let him take out a book on how to cure a cat's injured eye. He hated to give up this beautiful book, but now he had a real live cat and what was good for Old Cat came before anything else.

His microscope money, nineteen dollars and forty cents, was in a tin box that had held cough drops. His newly earned money—what was left after his own weekly needs and Old Cat's food were paid for—lay loose in a corner of the drawer. Of this, he left what he thought he'd need for cat food until Saturday's pay, and took all the rest—about a dollar and sixty or seventy cents. Then he locked the sideboard and set off on his bicycle.

The library was a small, old, pink-brick building with bay windows. It was set in a landscaped lawn on a shady street just off the main street of the town. He had gone there often before his keeping of the cat book had made him afraid to go back.

He went up to the desk and stood there for a moment, clutching the book; then he thrust it toward the clerk.

"Here, Miss," he said. "I kept this book too long. I can't afford to buy it, so I'm bringing it back. How much do I have to pay?"

The young clerk took the book, looked inside the cover, then beckoned to the librarian, who left her desk in the reading room and came over. She looked at Joel, then looked at the book, noticing the charging date and the overdue notices under the flap. Then she looked at Joel again.

"Why did you keep it so long?" she asked. "Why didn't you return it? You know, you could always borrow it again after a day or so."

"I–uh–I didn't have a cat then." Joel found it hard to explain. "I–well–I just kept looking at it, and–well–then it was too late."

"And now?"

"Now I have a cat. And I got to find out how to help him. Will I–do I have to pay it all at once? Could I take out just one book if I pay some money–now–and pay the rest later?"

The librarian still looked closely at him. She was perhaps in her early forties with short dark hair slightly graying. Her white blouse set off an olive skin deepened already with a touch of suntan. She smiled.

"I expect we'll be able to work out something," she said. "Did you know this book is an adult book? It is what people call a coffee-table book. But I'll just charge you the children's fine. That would be—let's see, that would be—uh—fifty cents."

"For *two* whole *years*?" Joel couldn't believe his luck. "Gee, I've got that much right here." He handed her the money, then asked, "And can I have a book that tells you what to do when a cat has a cut across his eye?"

"Oh—that sounds serious. Perhaps you'd better take your cat to a veterinarian. How did that happen?"

As she walked with him over to the bookshelves, Joel found himself telling her all about Old Cat, about how he had waited so long for him to come close, then the great overflow of love from the cat, and the remarkable matter of the kitten.

"He's really some cat, that Old Cat of mine," Joel told her. "He already had that cut–it was beginning to heal over–I don't know how he got it. It's all healed over in a scar now, but it looks like there's something wrong with his eye. I just don't know what to do."

The librarian chose two books, and they sat down at a table and looked them over. In the chapters on eye care, both books recommended that eye injuries be treated by the veterinarian.

"That costs a lot of money, don't it?" Joel said. "But I guess I can manage it for Old Cat." He chose one of the books to take home and study, so that he could learn more about caring for a cat.

"If you check that book in when it's due and leave it for a day, you may borrow it again if no one else has taken it out," the librarian reminded him; then she added, "I would dearly love to have a cat, but my husband is allergic to cats–some people are, you know."

"Yes, I know. My stepfather is. He says cats

give him asthma, and he won't let one come near him. He says–"

Joel stopped. Dad had been away for a year now. Would he ever come back, really, for good? He knew his mother received money from him, but he didn't think it was very much, or that it came very often. He had not thought of this before. What would happen to Old Cat–and the kitten–when–if Dad came back?

"You do have problems, don't you?" The librarian smiled at him. "Anyway, let's look in the telephone book for the veterinarian nearest you."

There were only two veterinarians listed in the telephone book. "I suppose a town this size is lucky to have two," she said as she copied the names and addresses and phone numbers on a card. "If you can't get either of them, I suppose you'd have to go all the way into the city. There is an animal shelter here, but–I don't know–I'm not sure what they do."

She wrote down the information about the animal shelter, also.

"If worst comes to worst, you can try that,"

she said. "But, it—well—it just might be a good idea to find out, first, what it's like."

She wished him good luck with Old Cat and Joel thanked her for all her help and pedaled home, trying to squash a little worm of fear that had begun to squirm inside him.

CHAPTER TWO

OLD CAT LAY FLAT ON THE GROUND FENDING OFF the bites and blows of the kitten who attacked his ears, his chin, his paws, until he rose and, with back arched and tail overhead, he circled her. She somersaulted and lay on her back, boxing with all four feet, then with all the force of her twelve ounces behind it, her left paw felled his sixteen pounds. He rolled over on his back, feet in the air.

When Joel opened the back door and came out into the yard, Old Cat cuffed the kitten away in earnest and wound himself around Joel's ankles.

Joel bent down and stroked his head and neck, and Old Cat, with hindquarters pressed against Joel's knee, rubbed his forehead on Joel's instep until, as usual, he fell over and rolled on the ground. The kitten bounded over and began to climb Joel's pantleg, and Old Cat, claws sheathed, grabbed Joel around the other ankle and held on.

"A guy can't even walk across his own yard anymore," Joel complained, laughing as he sat down on the ground and vainly tried to detach one cat after the other. He managed to pull a Ping-Pong ball out of his pocket and bounce it on the driveway. That took care of the kitten, and Old Cat, purring loudly, crawled onto his lap and nuzzled into the crook of his arm.

"I'm sure sorry about that eye, Old Cat," Joel said as he stroked the glossy fur. "But the vet says that you won't even notice when you go blind in it. He says it'll take awhile, and you'll get so used to looking out that other eye, you won't even know this'n don't work any more."

The worst part about the visit to the veterinarian had been getting Old Cat there. He had struggled, but finally gave in to being put in a box; but then Joel could not manage to hold the box on his bicycle. In the end he had wrapped Old Cat in the piece of old blanket and carried him, walking all the way there and back.

Even worse, perhaps, was listening to his mother afterwards.

"Well! I hope you're satisfied," she said. "All that money! You said you even spent some of your microscope money. For what? After you waiting half the afternoon, the doctor took five minutes to tell you there wasn't anything he could do for that cat's eye! All that time, all that money, for nothing—nothing! You want to throw away your hard-earned money on that old cat, don't expect me to back you up. And don't you ever—"

"But, Mom—"

"Why you have to—"

"But I *do* have to."

"Why?"

"Because—because well, I have to do whatever he needs—I gotta do whatever I can because

—because he has to depend on me—and I can't just *not* do it, can I?"

"At *that* price?"

Now, as Old Cat nudged and butted and rubbed against him, Joel thought he'd paid little enough. The change in Old Cat, from fighting tom, to this loving, playful animal was almost like a miracle. And Joel had not only watched it happen, but had helped to bring it about.

Today was Saturday. Joel had spent four hours this morning doing chores at the supermarket while Louella, the girl next door, baby-sat the Fiends. Friday and Saturday were his mother's busiest days at the beauty parlor; her free day was Monday. Joel had always, before Old Cat came to live with him, had half of Saturday for his own free time, but now, until school was out for the summer, he had to baby-sit on Saturday afternoons after he finished his job at the supermarket. As long as he stayed at home and kept a watchful eye on the Fiends, he was allowed to have a friend come to keep him company, and today Wayne was coming over. They were going to practice their basketball shots into the ring Dad had fixed on the garage over the driveway, before he had left for the city so long ago.

Wayne, the youngest of four brothers, was a year older than Joel and almost three inches taller. He was becoming a first-rate jump-shooter and was helping Joel try to improve his shooting and dunking. They spent an hour at practice, then after Joel split a popsicle for the Fiends, who were playing in the sandpile, they sat down on the back steps and opened the tall cans of soda that Wayne had brought.

"That Old Cat of yours—looks like he gets bigger and better-looking every time I see him," Wayne said after a long swallow of pop. As Old Cat came over and crawled into Joel's lap, Wayne went on, "He's sure a loving cat. I never seen an old tom so loving. You sure got him tamed." He reached over and stroked Old Cat, who nestled closer to Joel. "He ain't so scared of me as he used to be, but I don't think he takes too much to anybody but you."

Joel told Wayne about the trip to the veterinarian.

"It sure cost a lot of money, but I didn't have no choice. I called that animal shelter, but they don't have a doctor over there. I don't know what they really do."

"I do." Wayne spoke with disgust. "You want to keep away from there, man. All they got is a bunch of little cages, and they put the animals in there and feed them 'til they get too many. Sometime they get people to keep some, like a foster home, until they find homes for them. But even so most of the time they got more than they have room for. So about once a week, maybe, they crowd them into a kind of drum or some kind of a tank-thing and—well, *they* call it 'putting them to sleep.' "

"How you know all about it?" Joel asked. "You never took any of your dogs over there, did you?"

"No! And I never will."

He pulled on the soda again.

"My brother Leroy, just after he graduated from high school—he worked over there for a couple of weeks that summer. You know, all us kids, we always liked animals, and he thought he'd have a ball looking after a lot of dogs and cats and maybe learning what to do for them if they was sick or injured. Well, they don't do nothing like that. When people come there to get a dog or a cat, they supposed to have it fixed so they don't breed any more pups or kittens. They get a vet to operate on them for that, and sometimes he gives them shots or something, but only if somebody is going to take them home. Mostly, if they sick or injured, they just get put right into that—that thing—I think they call it some kind of a chamber."

"Golly!" Joel rubbed Old Cat under the chin. The kitten woke from where she had dropped to sleep and pranced over to the boys. Wayne picked her up and fondled her.

"Yeh. Leroy said it was bad enough when the animals was sick or hurting, but it was worse when they was lively and healthy. He had to see them get put into that—that chamber, cats and dogs together sometimes, and the guy who operated it used to laugh at all the screeching and hollering that went on in there before they was dead. At least—Leroy said that otherwise he seemed like a decent guy. Leroy thought maybe he just laughed because it kinda upset him, too."

"Man!" Joel was appalled. "I thought they was supposed to be humane. I seen a picture in the paper of some kittens they was giving away to a good home, and a dog somebody had adopted."

"I guess they figure they're being humane. They probably figure it don't matter if the animals suffer while they're getting—put to sleep—because when it's over, they'll be out of their misery. There's just too many animals nobody wants—any more—and in the summertime especially, they just can't keep them more'n a few days—there just ain't enough room. It's worse maybe here than some other places because of the lakes. People from away come on vacation and just leave their animals behind."

Both boys quietly drank their soda, thinking.

Then, "How long does it take?" Joel asked. "How long in that—chamber-thing before they're dead?"

"Leroy said he didn't know, really. The guy used to set it for ten or fifteen minutes. Leroy was supposed to help him pile up the dead animals, and then they buried them all together in a sort of pit. And one time one of the cats wasn't dead. The guy said it would have to go back in with the next batch. Otherwise it'd just get buried alive with the dead ones. That was when Leroy quit. He just walked out and came home and never even went back to get his pay. Seems like if all them animals have to be killed—'put to sleep,' like hell!—there ought to be a better—hey, there! Leave me a piece of my T-shirt to take home, huh?"

He tried to pull his T-shirt away from the kitten's teeth, then from each paw as she climbed over his chest and around his neck.

"Hey, Bitsy," he called. "Come rescue me from this little monster. And keep her off the driveway, please, so we can practice some more. OK?"

Bitsy took thc kitten to the far side of the yard, and when she dragged a piece of honeysuckle around in a circle, the kitten chased it. She played with Bitsy until she flopped, tired out, and slept again.

Old Cat sat sleek and handsome on the top of the back steps as the boys went back to their practice.

CHAPTER THREE

ANOTHER WEEK WENT BY, ANOTHER WEEK OF golden days and sweet-scented breezes. With the promise of school closing at its end, the week would have been perfect but for the bad news: Joel's job would now be turned over to an older teen-ager in a new program of "summer jobs for youth." He hoped he could find some other job soon because he needed the money. Even his microscope money was low. Bitsy and Seth would go to a summer nursery school, and he would have most of each summer day to himself. If they would let him in, he intended to join a nature-study group—he would be the youngest member—that went on field trips three days a week. The rest of the time he'd be on his own. This would be the first summer his mother had not made him attend a day camp, but she had finally agreed that this past year he had earned his freedom.

On Sunday evening they ate their supper of cold cuts and potato salad out in the back yard. The food was put out on a card table, but they sat on the ground, picnic fashion, and ate from paper plates. The car had been parked in front of the house so the Fiends could ride their tricycles in the driveway. Old Cat lay in a corner of the yard, the kitten, full-fed, asleep between his paws.

"Some day, God willing, we going to have a real patio, with a cookout grill and lounge chairs and a nice table with an umbrella over it and some nice plants and shrubs and flowers growing around." Joel's mother lighted her cigarette, then wrapped her arms around her knees and gazed out at the rich, velvety-dark treetops against the fading sunset over the lake.

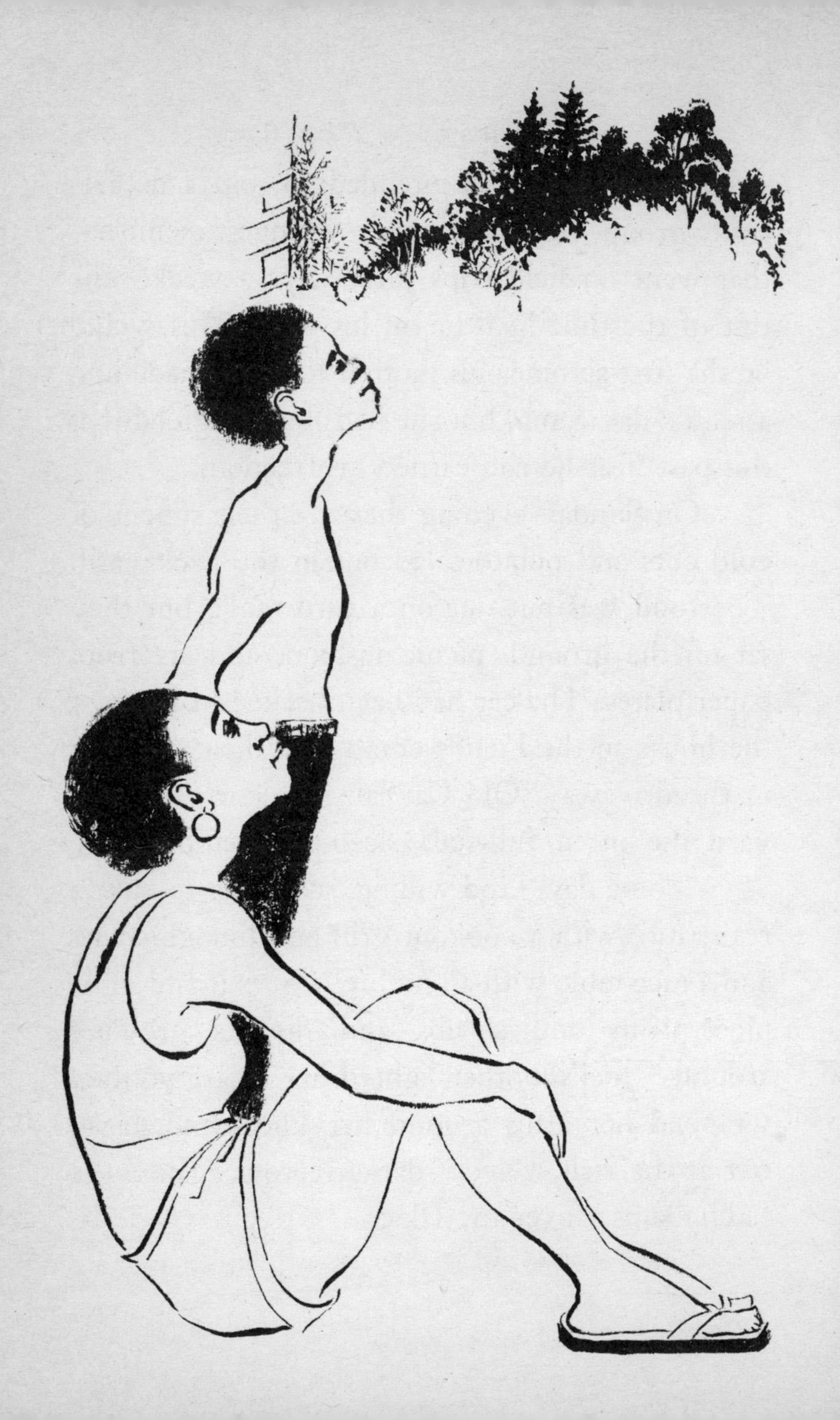

"And we'll be able to look out over the lake and not just see the tops of the trees around it."

"And I'll help with those plants and flowers," Joel promised. "Maybe even right here I can do something with that stuff growing along the back of the yard this summer. Maybe I can plant you a flowerbed. Maybe–"

"Yes 'maybe.' And 'someday'–"

The clang of the telephone from within the house interrupted her.

"Get it, will you, Joel? It's probably just a wrong number. If it's that old biddy wanting me to come in and give her a permanent on my free day tell her, 'No!' Politely."

Joel came running back almost at once.

"Hey, Mom! Guess what? It's Dad! Dad's on the phone. He says he's got good news for us. Hurry up!"

As his mother dashed past him, Joel looked out into the darkening yard. He could just make out the shape of Old Cat asleep with his chin over the kitten between his paws.

There wouldn't be much time–hardly

enough to get everything ready to go.

Dad wanted them there by next Friday, so that they'd have the whole weekend to get settled into their new home.

His new job in the chemical plant was permanent—as permanent as any job could be nowadays—and a house, partly furnished, was provided for them.

"You going to have your own room, Joel! And you can fix it any way you like. And Dad says the junior high school nearby is supposed to be one of the best schools in the city. He says he'll still be on wages for a while, but he's been promised a promotion and a good monthly salary, soon as another man retires. Maybe I can help out 'til then and get a chair in some beauty parlor over there. The company even runs a nursery school for a small fee."

It was late. The Fiends were asleep, and Joel and his mother were sitting as usual in front of the television, but they hadn't turned it on.

"Will there be a yard—a back yard?" Joel wanted to know.

"I suppose so. It probably won't be the patio of my dreams, no lake view or anything like that. But, oh Joel, I'm so happy! I don't care if we don't have fancy things—Dad wants us all to be with him! We'll have a real home again. Isn't that grand, Joel? Isn't it grand? I'm so happy!"

She was radiant. He had never thought about it before, but now Joel saw that his mother was really a beautiful woman.

"What you staring at, boy? I'm your mom, remember? And we're moving. We're going to a new home, with Dad in the city. What's the matter with you?"

Her world was full of riches; Joel's was full of loss. He knew before he spoke that what he feared was true and all his joy with Old Cat was coming to an end.

"I'm thinking about Old Cat, Mom," he said. "How we going to take him and the kitten; and where they gonna be—"

"Now you look here, Joel." His mother turned on him. "Don't you go spoiling all this on account of those cats. You know as well as I do we can't take them with us. You know that, Joel —now, don't you?"

"But Mom, they *our* cats! We responsible for them. You promised—"

"No! I never did promise. I was careful not to, in case something—in case Dad came back, or something."

"You mean—Mom, you mean you want us to—*abandon* them?"

The pain in Joel's voice, in his face, struck her and she sat silent, lips tight, searching for a way to ease his hurt.

Then, "We don't have much time, Joel." She tried to speak slowly, gently. "There's not much time—to see if you can find a home for those cats. I just don't see anybody wanting to take on that old cat. Tell you what we'll do: we'll put an ad in the paper. I'll divide the cost with you. But Joel—you responsible to me, too. And to the Fiends, and to Dad. Besides, I'm going to need you to help me get things sorted and packed, and got rid of. I won't be thinking much about cats from now on."

"Not even the kitten, Mom? I thought—I thought you liked having that kitten. You said you wanted your own pet."

"Sure, I liked the kitten, but it's not as important to me. I got other things now to worry about—it's just not important to me, now."

"You important to it, Mom. It's got to live and have a home, too."

"Go on, Joel! You talk like cats were people. They're cats, and cats can take care of themselves."

"Yeh—like they was when Old Cat came around. Like the kitten was, half-dead when Old Cat brought her—"

"I told you I'd go halves with you on an ad in the paper. There ought to be somebody in this town that'll take them—at least the kitten."

"So Old Cat got to lose his home and his friends and his kitten—where's all his love going to go?"

"He won't be any worse off than he was before. Come on now, we got to get to bed. We got to get up early in the morning and get moving—

really get moving, hey—right?"

Joel didn't answer. He lay awake on the sofa long after his mother had gone to bed, thinking about Old Cat, trying to hope that somebody would take care of him, see that he was fed. But would that be enough? If Old Cat could react to kindness with so much love, could he not feel the hurt of being unwanted and abandoned? If cats could love, couldn't they also grieve?

Perhaps the folks who would move into their house after they left might feed Old Cat and let him stay. But suppose they wouldn't? Or had dogs? And how long would it be before people moved in?

Hours passed before Joel, exhausted, turned over on his stomach and fell asleep.

CHAPTER FOUR

THERE WERE NOT MANY CALLS IN ANSWER TO Joel's ad in the paper. There were just too many kittens and puppies and not enough homes, so that his ad was only one of many for animals being given away, free.

"You don't have to pay/If you're giving them away!" the clerk chanted when Joel asked how much the ad would cost. Nobody wanted Old Cat. Some people who wanted a kitten wouldn't take a black one; some held out for a Siamese or part-Siamese. One person wanted a black kitten but wouldn't take a female.

At the bottom of the newspaper ad column was a note in bold face type:

IF YOU DON'T SUCCEED IN PLACING YOUR ANIMAL IN A GOOD HOME, LET US HELP YOU.

This was followed by the name and address of the local animal shelter.

"Looks like you might have to take them over there, Joel. That is, if you don't want to leave them loose to take their own chances and take care of themselves."

"No! At least, I wouldn't ever take Old Cat there. The kitten might be safe for a few days, but not Old Cat."

Joel told his mother what Wayne had told him about the animal shelter.

"I don't believe it!" his mother retorted. "There's a picture in the paper every week of animals they find homes for or rescue or something. You hadn't ought to take his word for a thing like that. Maybe that kid needs to have his mouth washed out with soap."

She was just leaving to deliver the Fiends to

summer nursery school, then go to work.

"I'll be home early this afternoon, maybe by lunchtime. My last appointment is this permanent at nine-thirty." She stood silent for a moment then, "Time's running out on us, Joel," she said. "We only got one more day. And we need to get everything ready to put in that U-Haul by tomorrow afternoon. We want to be out on the road by sunup on Friday."

They had put a sign out in the front yard:

FURNITURE AND HOUSEHOLD GOODS
FOR SALE—CHEAP

and had disposed of some things in exchange for a little money. Dad had said not to bring much—only a few things that they just didn't want to part with—because the company house had most of what they'd need. Most of their things were old and shabby. The few unsold, unwanted items, things for which there would be no room in the U-Haul, such as Joel's old sofa, would simply be left behind.

Whenever people came to look at their stuff,

Joel and his mother tried to interest them in taking the cats, but nobody wanted cats now. The kitten was admired, but no home was offered for her.

Joel hated the comments some of the people made, and the attitude of many of them about cats:

Kittens are cute, but they grow up to be cats, and who needs cats? Not poor people for sure. When they get to be cats you'd better turn them out to fend for themselves. They've got nine lives. They can take care of themselves. It costs too much to have them operated on to stop them from having more kittens. All you have to do is wait until there are too many strays all over the neighborhood, then call the State Pest Control. They'll come and exterminate them, same as they do other varmints. When there are so many, too many, it's only common sense to put them out of their misery.

Cats—cats full of love like Old Cat. Common sense—common sense, maybe. But it's not right! It's just not right, Joel thought.

Joel searched until he found the newspaper ad and the telephone number of the local animal shelter.

"Yes, may I help you?" The voice was that of a young woman, soft and gracious.

"I wanted to ask you–about cats–and kittens."

"Oh, we have some adorable kittens up for adoption–almost every kind and color you could want. Can you come in?"

"No–I mean–I wanted to ask you if you'd take in a cat, and a kitten."

"Oh. Well–we're terribly crowded right now. I'm afraid we wouldn't be able to keep the cat very long. We might be able to keep the kitten a little longer–kittens have a better chance of being adopted, you know. But we're really awfully full–"

"What do you do . . . when you . . . when you get too full?"

"Well, of course, when there's no more room, when we simply can't keep them any longer, we have no choice. We have to put them to sleep. But we do keep them just as long as we possibly can."

"Miss, I want to know how. *How* you put them to sleep."

"Oh we use the very latest method. It's quick, painless—it's the method used by many animal shelters and humane societies all over the country."

"But *how*—what is it?"

"You mean, how does it work?"

"Yes."

"Well, it's called a decompression chamber, and the animals are put—yes? Yes? Are you on the line?"

Joel thought of Old Cat in that death-trap. He broke out in perspiration and dropped the receiver back on the cradle.

He'd have to let him go. He'd just have to leave Old Cat to take his chances, to fend for himself and struggle again for his own survival. Anything was better than that chamber.

Old Cat would have to be abandoned again.

And Joel would never know how Old Cat made out, whether or not he survived, or how. Or whether somebody would take pity on him and give him a home. That would not be easy; it would be more trouble and effort than most people were willing to spend, especially on a cat, an old cat, a cat with a disfigured face and one eye going blind. And Joel would never know if he got picked up and ended up in that chamber after all—or had to be put in twice.

Joel was throwing up in the bathroom when the telephone rang. By the time he reached it, the ringing had stopped. He waited a few minutes, then dialed the number of the beauty parlor where his mother worked.

"Mom? Did you call a little while ago? No, I was . . . I was in the bathroom."

"Listen carefully, Joel. And write down this name and address on a piece of paper. Ready?"

"Wait a sec, Mom. The Fiends must have got hold of that pad again—OK, I got it."

"Mrs. Avery Grant." She spelled it all out. "Two fourteen Laurel Road, Apartment Three

C. Got it? You know where Laurel Road is—it's just one block west of the library, and Mrs. Grant lives in that apartment house two blocks south of there. She's just moved in and her phone isn't in yet so you'll have to bicycle over there. Why? My customer says Mrs. Grant just might take the kitten. She's my customer's sister-in-law —no! Not Old Cat, just the kitten. She's just sold her home and moved in there and she'll be living all by herself. She's always had a cat 'til her old cat died awhile back. Well, anyway—don't take the kitten 'til we know, but get on over there and see her right away. Tell her Mrs. Carney—Mrs. Blanche Carney sent you. You got it? You got everything straight? OK, I'll see you later."

Joel put the slip of paper in his back pocket and went out the back door. Old Cat uncurled himself and stretched and yawned and came over to Joel. He did his old trick of pressing his tail end against Joel's leg with his forehead on Joel's instep until he fell over on his back, feet in the air. Joel rarely picked him up, but now he gath-

ered Old Cat up in his arms and buried his face in the cat's neck.

"What I gonna do with you, Old Cat? What I gonna *do*? And how you gonna understand I mean well for you? I don't want you hurt no more. I just don't know what to do; I just don't know."

The small apartment house was neatly set on a tidy lawn with well trimmed hedges and a few flowering shrubs.

Joel found Mrs. Grant's name and apartment number over a button which he pressed. There was a crackling noise and a voice which seemed to sputter, "Who's there? Who is it?" He spoke into a small, round thing.

"Joel—Joel Dennison. Mrs. Blanche Carney sent me. I come to see you about a kitten."

"Blanche? Kitten? Did you say kitten?"

"Yes, a kitten."

"Come on up—third floor."

When Joel reached the third floor he stood for a moment wondering which of the six doors belonged to 3C. The one nearest the elevator opened and a woman looked out.

"Oh–I thought you sounded like a boy. Come in, young man, come in."

CHAPTER FIVE

JOEL ENTERED A LARGE ROOM THAT SEEMED beautiful to him, although several cartons stood around on the floor and pictures, mostly in heavy frames, were not hung, but stacked against the wall. A piano stood against one wall and the furniture had a solid, rich, comfortable look. Mrs. Grant had been hanging her drapes, which were heavy and full.

"Would you like to give me a hand? I'm not as good a climber as I used to be."

Joel stood up on a stepstool and fastened the

hooks onto the rod. She pulled the cord and the drapes opened and closed gracefully. She pulled them open again as Joel stepped down.

"Thank you—that's just great. What did you say your name is?"

Joel told her his name again and explained about his mother's call from the beauty parlor.

"Sit down, Joel, and tell me all about this kitten," Mrs. Grant said as she went into the kitchen. She returned with cans of soda, glasses and cookies on a tray, which she set down on the coffee table. She poured the soda into the tall glasses and handed one to Joel with a little napkin. He sat on the sofa and she sat on a small chair facing him.

She was a small woman, rather plump, with blue-white hair cut short and straight, and she was wearing a light blouse over slacks. Her eyes, large and deep blue, were fixed on Joel as he described the kitten.

"She's black with a few little white hairs on her shoulder, just like Old Cat . . ." He stopped and looked down into his glass.

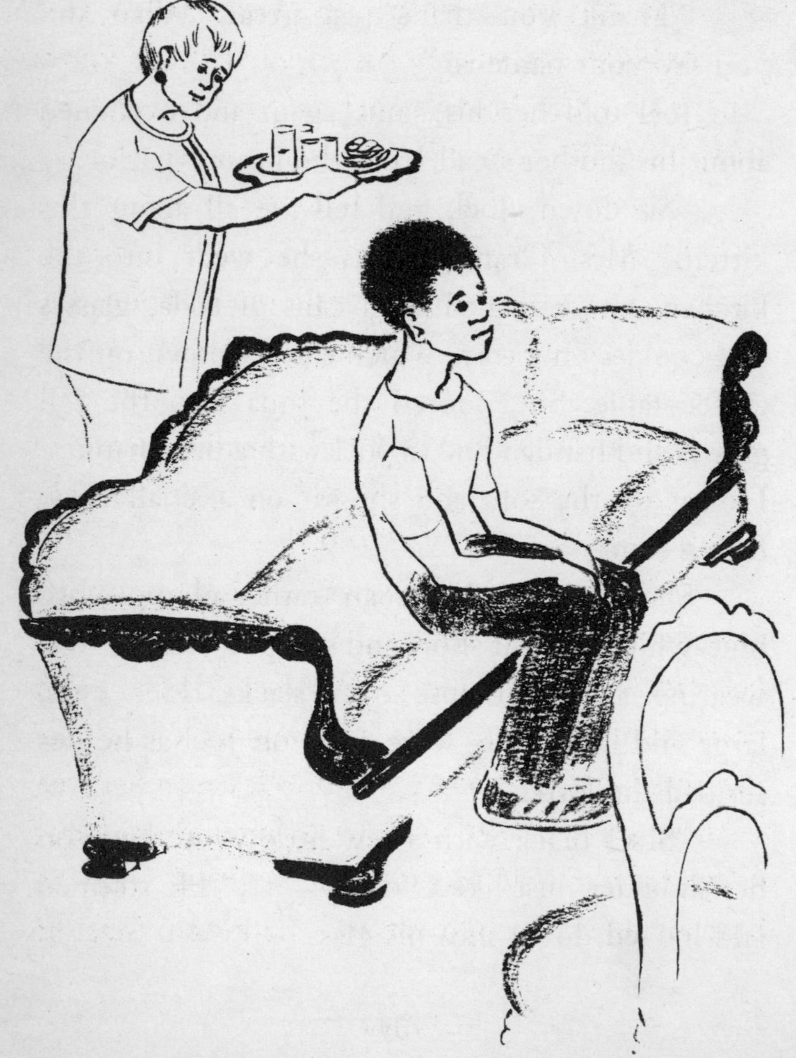

"How old is she?"

"I don't really know," Joel looked up again. "I guess she's about two, maybe three months. She was maybe six-seven weeks old when Old Cat brought her to me, half-dead. I don't know where Old Cat brought her *from*, but I'm sure she's his child—they're just exactly alike."

"*His*?"

"Yes. Old Cat is a tom. He's the lovingest cat! He was wild at first, scared and starving. He used to hiss and talk back—sounded just like he was swearing."

He set his glass down and leaned forward.

"Mrs. Grant—please—can't you, *please* will you give Old Cat a home, too?"

"Oh, Joel," she answered. "I wish I could—I really do! But, Joel, you know I could never keep an old wild tom in an apartment house. He'd go crazy if I tried to keep him indoors. I can take the kitten—she's young enough to learn to become a house cat and get used to living indoors. But never an old tom. But tell me more—I want to hear all about that old cat and the kitten. Start at the beginning, when you first found Old Cat—or when he found you."

In spite of the hurt inside him, Joel began to tell about Old Cat, and as he talked he found comfort in the telling, in reliving the joy of Old Cat's love, his amazing behavior with the kitten.

"I just don't know what to do. Nobody wants Old Cat. My mother and my stepfather won't let me take him when we move—Dad's allergic to cats. Looks like I'll just have to go off and leave him. I think he was abandoned before, and now he'll have to hunt and fight and steal to survive again. And he's getting older and one of his eyes is going blind. He had a great big cut over it when I found him. Everybody says cats can take care of themselves, but I think it must be awful hard for them. He sure was in bad shape and so was the kitten. I just can't stand to think of him like that again. And how's he gonna think of me—"

He pressed his lips together and shook his head.

"You do love that cat, don't you," Mrs. Grant said. "I do wish I could help. I agree with you about abandoned cats. It's cruel, downright cruel. I have several friends who love cats and who might take another. But an old tom who has never lived inside could be a real problem. And the shelter isn't the answer, is it? They try, but there are always too many stray pets and too little money, too little space. In other places they do better, but not here, not yet anyway. Joel," she leaned toward him and put her hand on his knee. "Joel, have you thought about having Old Cat put to sleep?"

"I can't! I just can't do it. I've thought and thought, but I can't let them do that to Old Cat."

Mrs. Grant rose from her chair and went over to the stack of pictures leaning against the wall. She tipped them each forward until she came to the fourth one which was a long panel with three large full-color photographs.

"Come here and help me get this out," she said. "We'll set it on the sofa for the time being.

I want you to see these pictures of *my* old cat."

Joel helped her draw the panel out and set it on the sofa.

"I had these made from snapshots. Oh, I loved that cat the way you love your old cat. His name was Barney and was he smart! Do you know, that cat could open doors? And drawers?"

The photographs showed a big gray-striped tabby with beautiful dark markings and enormous gray-green eyes. The center picture was like a portrait, with the cat sitting, looking into the camera, sleek, superior and dignified. One picture showed him admiring himself in a mirror. The third showed him looking up into a lamp as though he were examining the light socket.

"I had to have that fixture changed," she told Joel. "Barney used to pull the chain to make the light go on and off. After he tilted the whole thing over on himself I had the chain removed and a button put there. He never could understand that the chain was really gone. The button defeated him, but he never gave up looking for that chain."

"He sure a good-looking cat," Joel said. "He must have been mighty smart, too."

"Yes," she pulled up another small chair and they both sat down again and looked at the pictures on the sofa. "He was a great cat. We lived in a house in the city and I never let him prowl the neighborhood. He was an 'inside' cat, but I had a leash for him and took him outside now and then. He used to open the drawer and pull the leash out of it and drag it to me when he wanted to go out on the lawn. I'll do the same with the kitten. She'll soon adapt to being an inside cat. It's safer for cats nowadays to be kept indoors."

"You musta really took–taken–good care of him, taking his picture and all that."

"Yes. I suppose he was spoiled. The children loved him and when they grew up and left home, my husband and I spoiled him even more. And when my husband died two years ago, Barney was a great comfort to me although he was ailing."

"Gee–he musta been an awful old cat."

"Yes, he'd always had such good care he lived to be almost twenty years old."

"What—what made him—die?"

"When he began to suffer and couldn't move much—when his hind legs wouldn't work for him anymore, I had him put to sleep."

Joel stared at her.

"You mean—you loved that old cat so much —and you let them do *that* to him? You let your old cat get put into that *chamber*?"

"Oh, no, Joel. No! Not a decompression chamber! I didn't think he deserved that. No animal does. Did you know that the decompression chamber has been outlawed in some states? Unfortunately, our isn't one of them. No, Joel. I took him to the vet. I held him in my arms while the doctor gave him a needle. I stroked him and talked to him, and Barney didn't even know he'd had a needle. He just went to sleep, in my arms—for good."

Mrs. Grant promised to drive over to Joel's house after supper to pick up the kitten after she'd made things ready for her, and Joel bicycled slowly home.

CHAPTER SIX

"WHERE IN BLAZES YOU BEEN, JOEL? HERE, IT'S pushing three o'clock, and I've got all this packing to do and no sign of you around to give me any help. Did you go over to that old lady's place? That was about ten o'clock this morning I called you. Answer me, Joel! What you been up to anyway?"

Joel stood in the doorway, the piece of old blanket trailing from his hand. He did not look at his mother and he did not answer.

"You going to answer me or not?" She put

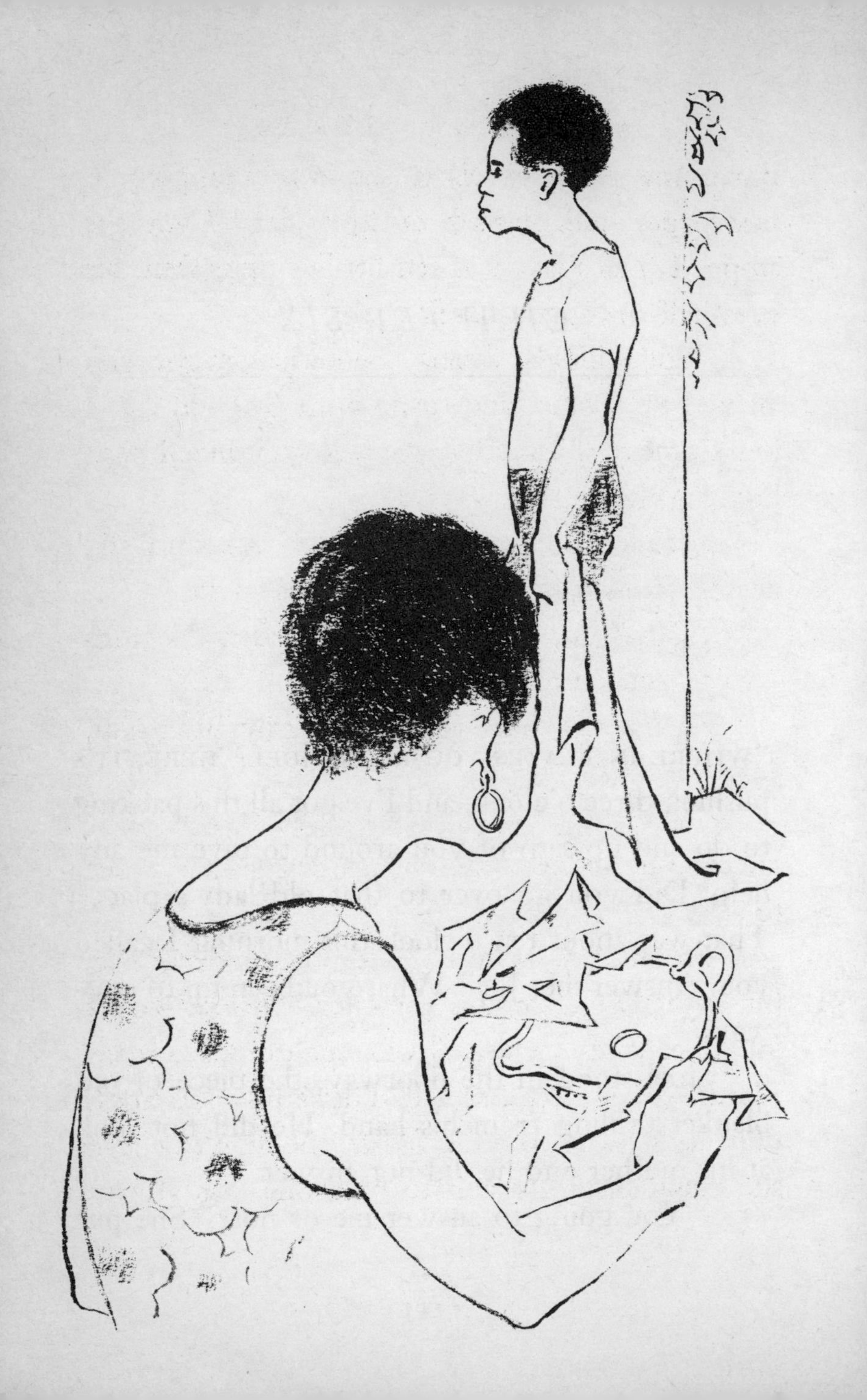

down the piece of china she was wrapping in newspaper and started toward Joel. Then she stopped. Joel's jaw was set, his lips tight shut, his eyes half-open, and blank.

"Something's wrong. Something's got you all tied up. Something to do with that old cat, I bet. Come to think, I haven't seen him since I been home. Where is he?"

"Under the roses—under the roses in the alley." Joel's lips barely moved as he spoke.

"What you talking about? Under the roses —what you mean?"

So quietly that she could hardly hear him, Joel told her.

"You mean, you spent all the rest of your microscope money just to have that old cat put to sleep?"

He did not answer. He did not look at her, but as she looked at him, she knew what he would look like when he was older, much older, a man. Hard. No, not hard, strong. That kind of strength must have come from his father; she didn't believe she could have given it to him. She was always too pushed, too tired trying to cope with the Fiends, with her job and making ends meet. Maybe when they got to their new place. . . .

"I'm sorry, Joel. I'm sorry. I do wish you didn't take these kind of things so hard. There—I'm sorry."

She stood at his side and put both arms around his shoulders and laid her cheek on his forehead.

"I'm so sorry."

He pulled away from her and walked, without speaking, across the kitchen into the living room.

The old sofa, the only remaining piece of furniture in the living room, stood on the rugless floor, solitary in the center of the room.

Joel lay on his back, arms crossed on his chest, knees drawn up, and stared at the bare spot on the ceiling, the spot shaped like a mouse sitting on its haunches.

The kitten came out from under the sofa and jumped up beside him. He stroked her, noting how, when he drew his hand across her back, her hind quarters rose—just like Old Cat's. Just like Old Cat. He drew her up to his chest and she began to lick him, under his chin, around his ears, trying to nuzzle under his head and back of his neck. She was plump and warm and silky and—thanks to Old Cat—alive.

He took her in both hands and held her up above his face.

"You gonna be all right," he whispered. "I promise you—*you* gonna be all *right*."

Then he turned over on his stomach and found that he could let them out—tears, not sobs. They flowed easily, pouring out comfort, and the kitten, between his shoulder and his cheek, licked them away as they fell.